Security Agent's Alien Bartender

Olympus Station, Volume 3

Aurelia Skye

Published by Amourisa Press, 2020.

Blurb

AGENT EMILY IPSY IS determined to make a name for herself. That leads to unauthorized shifts and sneaking around. She keeps running into Anthracite, the bartender. If he's really just a bartender, why is he everywhere—and why can't she stop thinking about him?

Anth is stationed at Olympus Station on assignment from his government. He's there to do a job, but Emily keeps getting in his way. She's maddening, distracting, and pure temptation. He needs to keep his eyes on the job and hands off the security agent, but that's proving impossible. When an old enemy of his people surfaces, he'll need Emily's help to find out why Baatesh is there and stop what he's doing. After working with her at his side, will he ever want to let her go?

Chapter One

IT WAS LATE AT NIGHT or early in the morning, depending on one's perspective. Though Emily Ipsy, Olympus Station security agent, was technically off duty, she was still monitoring the situation closely.

The *situation* being Anthracite, ostensibly just the bartender at the bar on the promenade deck, but she was starting to suspect he was more. She kept seeing him turn up wherever she was, though she was certain he wasn't following her. She was sure he had no idea she was trailing or observing him.

She wasn't officially authorized to do so, but with her resolve to be promoted, she was determined to find something that could help her with that goal. If she could stop a crime before it happened or bring someone dangerous like Anthracite to the attention of Commander Templeton, it could only help her ambitions.

What had started out as a general all-purpose mission to ensure everything was as it should be had narrowed down over the past few weeks to focus on Anthracite. The man was everywhere, and he'd drawn her suspicion.

She followed him now, easily picking him out among the people crowding the club. Most beings were interested in hooking up or unwinding, but there was an air of purpose about Anthracite that added to her suspicions. She followed discreetly, trying to keep enough distance between them that he wouldn't realize he was being followed while not risking losing him. With his distinctive red skin and red-black horns, she wasn't likely to anyway.

She stumbled to a stop, quickly darting behind a canoodling throuple when Anthracite stopped at a table, sitting down with one of his own kind. There usually weren't many diabels on Olympus Station, so two of them together was enough to pique her interest. Lifting her wrist comm, she used it to record a video of the two of them together, wishing she were close enough to pick up what they were talking about to record that as well.

Whatever the meeting was about, and it certainly didn't seem to be anything but a meeting, it was over quickly. Anthracite said something to which the other man responded before passing over what looked like a small case. Emily was certain it was a data chip, having seen those cases all her life.

She was dying to know what was on it, so she waited until Anthracite had left his meeting, slipping through the dance club several paces behind him. It was going to be harder to follow him once they were out of the club, so she waited near the entrance for a tick, though afraid to wait too long and lose track of him.

As she darted out, she looked first of the left and then to the right, seeing the red flash of his tail as he turned down the corridor. She quickly went that direction, though trying to maintain a casual distance. She slipped down the corridor he had followed, looking for him, and once again saw a flash of his tail as he turned to the left farther down.

She waited a moment before following him, hoping she didn't miss him.

When she rounded the corner of that corridor, she looked around and saw nothing. She frowned in confusion, since there was nothing but storerooms around her. If she recalled correctly from the schematics, this was a storage area for the businesses and shops on the promenade, and as she started to read the doors, the one labeled for the bar opened, revealing Anthracite.

She started to think of a pretext, or simply just nod and walk by, but before she could, his tail snaked out, wrapped around her waist, and jerked her inside the room with him. The door closed a moment later, and she pressed her back against it.

Fear crept over her, making her respiration increase and her heartrate rise. She stared up at him in shock, licking her lips as she braced herself for him to hurt her.

He leaned closer, and there was definitely an edge of menace about him, so it was a surprise when his tone was perfectly pleasant as he said, "I'm flattered that you keep following me, Agent Ipsy. If you wish to mate, you only have to ask."

Her eyes widened, and she gasped in outrage. How dare he proposition her? Even worse, if she didn't follow the cue he was giving her, she risked blowing her entire operation and losing all the time she'd spent following him. She opened her mouth. "I..."

"Are you shy? Perhaps you think I'm not interested in humans? You'll find I have eclectic tastes, Agent Ipsy." He leaned closer, trailing a knuckle down her cheek. "Or should I call you Emily?"

She licked her lips again, nerves assailing her. She was uncertain how to respond. He was giving her the perfect opening to pretend like she hadn't been following him, or at least not for the reason he suspected, but could she really go through with it? Could she fake an attraction to him?

Who was she kidding? There'd be nothing fake about it. This close to him, it was impossible not to admire what a beautiful creature he was, with his stunning features, rock-hard and well-defined body, and thick arms that could easily crush her. For some reason, that thought was mildly delightful, but only in a sexual context of course. "Emily is fine."

"She certainly is." With a chuckle, he moved closer, grasping her hip with a hand as his tail pulled her against him. "Very fine indeed."

"What should I call you? I don't know your last name."

He smiled. "Just Anthracite or Anth will do."

She tipped her head slightly. "But what is your last name? I'd like to know." It could be pertinent for an investigation of him, though now that she thought about it, she didn't recall seeing his last name listed on any of his personnel files that she'd accessed through legitimate means.

"Diabels aren't big on last names, sweet Emily." His mouth came closer, grazing her cheek. "Besides, you only need to know one name, don't you?"

She hesitated. "I suppose?" That came out sounding more like a question than an answer, and she shivered when his lips brushed her cheek.

"You just need to know what to call out when you come around my cock, don't you?"

Emily gasped, no longer able to keep up the pretense. He was attractive, but he could also be a criminal, and there was no way she was going to sleep with him just to keep it quiet that she was investigating him. "You're so rude."

She put her hands on his chest and shoved, moving him backward. She suspected he let her go as easily as he moved. She put her hands on her hips, her fingers brushing against her taser. She kept her fingers well away from it, feeling no need to draw it at the moment. "You might as well know I'm on to you."

He tilted his head slightly. "You're not yet, but you could be." His eyes gleamed, making her realize they were just black pupils and irises surrounded by pale red sclera. It was unusual and striking, but it fit with the rest of the man.

She glared at him. "Enough. I keep seeing you sneak around Olympus Station, and I demand to know what you're doing."

He seemed unbothered by her accusation. He just grinned at her again. "Oddly enough, I've seen you doing the same thing, Agent Ipsy. You've been my little shadow for days now, but it's not just me you follow. You poke around everywhere, including places where it isn't your business."

Her eyes widened at his knowledge. "Are you investigating me?"

He chuckled then. "No, and I couldn't care less what you're doing as a rule, except when it involves me. Why are you following me?" As he asked, he put both his hands on the door, pushing her against it again and holding her with his body. He wasn't holding her tightly, but there was definitely a sense of confinement.

"If you're not after my body, what is it you want, Emily?" He brought his mouth forward, his lips once again teasing her cheek and making her shiver. "I suspect my body might be part of the package." As he chuckled, he thrust forward slightly, revealing the full length of his hard cock as he swept it against the juncture of her thighs in a brief touch before moving away.

Emily stiffened at the words even as her panties grew damp. She glared at him, though she couldn't deny the physical reaction sweeping through her. "You're doing something."

"Not at the moment."

She glared at him. "I don't know what you're up to, but you're surely creeping around, and who is that man you met with tonight?"

"I don't feel I can give you an explanation, Emily. The next time you follow me, you'd better be sure what you want, and just know I'm ready to give it to you whenever you're begging for it." With those words, his lips touched hers.

Emily meant to push him away. She put her hands against his chest with the intention of doing so, but somehow, she ended up grabbing his shirt and holding him against her, dragging him closer as his lips pressed to hers. His mouth sealed over hers, his tongue darting in between the seams of her lips to steal a taste of her.

She thought about biting him, but before she could decide either way, her teeth made the decision and were holding his tongue captive. It wasn't a hard bite though, and it wasn't intended to inflict pain. Well, maybe a little pain, but the pleasurable kind.

He growled low in his throat before pulling back from her. "Careful what promises you make that you aren't prepared to keep, Emily. I would never force you to do anything you don't want to, but it's not nice to lead a man on."

"I'm not leading you anywhere, except maybe to the brig." She was struggling to restore her composure now, telling herself she was angry that he had violated her in such a fashion. "Stay away from me, Anthracite."

He dipped his head in a pseudo-respectful fashion, though his lips were twitching. "I can do that, but the question is... Can you stay away from me, Emily?" With a wink, he stepped back from her, using his tail to move her aside before it unwound from her waist, and he passed through the door. He didn't look back as he left, turning right down the corridor.

For a moment, Emily considered following him, but she was too shaken by the experience. What had she been thinking, allowing him to kiss her? She hadn't even just allowed it. She had practically begged for it, clinging to him, and her bite hadn't been one to get him to free her. It had simply been to test his boundaries.

She shook her head at her own stupidity and hormonal urges. It had been a while since she'd taken a lover, because she was focused on advancing in her career and looking out for Olympus Station. This foolishness meant she needed to rectify that. Yes, she could go back to the club she had just been in and no doubt find an alien or human with whom to spend the night, but the idea held no appeal.

Telling herself she didn't want to sleep with anyone, while firmly blocking any thought of Anthracite from entering her mind, she marched out of the bar's storage room and down the corridor, taking the lift to her room.

When she disembarked on the lesser crew quarters' deck, she went to the small room that housed her, locking the door securely behind her while entertaining the idea of Anthracite following her. She should be fearful of the prospect, not shivering with anticipation at the idea of him pounding on her door, demanding to be let in so he could sweep her off to bed.

"I certainly don't want that." Saying it aloud almost made it true, and she went to the comm station in the corner. "Computer, look up files for Anthracite. Authorization Tao Beta one-one-four-two."

"The files are presently loading, Agent Ipsy," said the pleasant female voice of the computer. Seconds later, her screen filled with images and data.

Emily had seen it all before when she first became suspicious of him, and there was nothing there. There was nothing to indicate a problem, but mainly, there was just no data in general. The report from his home world, which was a member of the Coalition, showed a bland background with little substance. It included some education and job history, and a clean background check. Everything was so clean in fact that it raised her suspicions as it had before.

This time, she couldn't deny the urge to get more data. "Computer, call Venathi Sarwa at Coalition HQ. Oh, her private quarters." No doubt, Venathi was asleep.

It took more than a minute for the computer to establish a connection, and when Venathi appeared, she'd clearly been sleeping. She looked none too happy to be awoken, even though she and Emily were best friends from their academy days. "You'd better have a really good reason for waking me up. I had the most pleasant dream. I was being pleasured by two jrojs, a tarsa, and a human." She yawned.

"I guess it's not an emergency, but it's discreet."

Venathi nodded. "Channel eight-eight-four-two."

Emily didn't bother to ask the computer to adjust for her. It was just as simple to do it herself, and she accessed the control panel to change to a different comm channel. This one was secured and regularly swept for bugs. She could trust Venathi to maintain a confidential line, since her friend specialized in covert operations for the Coalition.

"What do you need?"

"I need everything you can find about Anthracite."

Venathi yawned and then started typing. A moment later she said, "What's the last name?"

"No last name. It appears diabels don't normally use surnames."

"Oh, he's a diabel? How fascinating. There are just so few of them left after the horrible war with the angrills, aren't there?" Venathi blinked, and Emily could see her thoughts returning to the task at hand. "It'll take me a while, since I have to do this discreetly. I'll get back to you as soon as I can."

"Thanks, Venathi. Sorry I woke you from that delicious dream. I hope you can get back to your jrojs, tarsa, and human."

Venathi chuckled. "So do I, dear friend." With those words, the screen went dark.

Chapter Two

EMILY FELT LIKE SHE was on tenterhooks as she waited for a reply from Venathi, which finally came through two days later. She'd been torn between avoiding Anthracite and following him, and she'd decided to error on the side of caution for now.

She was still observing him by visiting the bar and keeping him under surveillance in well populated areas, but she wasn't going to follow him alone again until she knew more about him. She was all too afraid he would collect on the promise she might've inadvertently issued, though it was all strictly physical.

She reviewed the information, annoyed by what she saw. It was all basically a duplicate of what she already had in front of her, available through the comm station. There was one simple note from Venathi, and it read: *I couldn't turn up anything. He's either clean or he's been cleaned.*

She could well imagine that meant either Anthracite had lived an exemplary life, or someone of immense power was cleaning up behind him and hiding anything they didn't want the Coalition to know. She considered that a far more likely prospect, and she could no longer hold off confronting him. If he meant harm to her station, she had to act.

Emily went to her personal armory, switching out the taser for the laser pistol. She didn't normally carry it, but it felt warranted this time, since she planned to confront Anthracite.

Once she was dressed and wearing her gun, she left her quarters and went first to the bar. She was disappointed to see a flenniken working the bar this evening, her bright pink plumage and sharp yellow beak immediately catching the eye. Emily rushed over to her, asking, "Is Anthracite working tonight?"

"Not right now," said the flenniken.

"Do you know when he'll be in?"

The bartender stopped for a moment to give her a look of disbelief. "Most of us don't want to hang out here unless it's for work, Agent Ipsy."

No, she could well imagine they didn't. It would be akin to her hanging out in the meeting room set aside for the security agents in the control hub. She nodded her thanks and left the bar, soon returning to the promenade.

She moved to a discreet corner before lifting her wrist comm. "Computer, locate Anthracite."

"Anthracite is in his quarters."

Emily headed that way, needing to take the lift to reach it the fastest.

It was only as she stepped out on the right deck, her stomach squeezing with dread, that she realized she was about to confront him. He might be quite dangerous, and she considered calling for backup for a moment.

She held back though. It wasn't from a sense of pride, or wanting to collar him herself. Her investigation was unauthorized, so she'd have to explain both to her partner Gordon Hayes and to the commander why she'd been following him during her off time, and why she was digging into his background.

She might even have to admit to involving Venathi, a blatant violation of Coalition laws. No, she had to handle this alone. If she found something truly adverse, she would report it to the commander and damn the consequences to her career or freedom, but she didn't want to be premature in reporting something that might not even be happening and risk her future.

She swallowed the lump in her throat and approached his door, banging instead of using the ringer. It opened seconds later, almost as if he'd been waiting for her. She gasped when she realized he was wearing only a towel wrapped around his hips, and there wasn't much of it. She pointedly looked over his shoulder. "I need to talk to you."

He seemed smug as he moved aside so she could step through the open door. It closed behind her with a hydraulic hiss a moment later that felt like it was sealing her doom.

Dismissing the flights of fancy, she turned to face him with her hand blatantly on the butt of her pistol. "I know you're up to something. I have new data about you. Who's cleaning up after you and keeping your record so spotless?"

"Emily, you don't have to keep inventing these pretexts to see me. I've already indicated I'm as attracted to you as you are to me." He looked down, blatantly illustrating his erection when her gaze dropped there. If not for the towel, she would've seen everything.

Her mouth watered at the thought, even as she took a step back. "I'm warning you. I'm watching you, and I want to know what you're doing around the station."

"I don't mean any harm to anyone." That seemed to be his only concession to her question.

"You're going to tell me—" She reached out to grab his shoulder as he started to turn away from her. In seconds, she found his arms around her, his tail holding her tightly against him again. As he took her into his arms, part of her acknowledged this was what she'd been hoping for when she'd reached out for him.

Instead of answering, his mouth descended on hers in a hungry kiss. Her mouth was just as avid, lips opening to accept his tongue as she stroked it with her own. She nipped his lower lip, making him chuckle, but this time, he didn't pull away. Instead, he lifted her, pressing her back against the door. Her legs wrapped around his hips, and she was vaguely aware of the towel dislodging as it slid down her leg before hitting the floor.

In her rational brain, she knew she was standing in the naked diabel's arms, but the animalistic side of her only reveled in the knowledge. She couldn't resist grinding against him as he pressed the full heat of his arousal against her folds. His mouth continued to devour hers, and she was eagerly meeting each thrust of his tongue with her own. Her fingers clenched, nails digging into his shoulders, which made him purr with satisfaction.

Emily was ashamed to admit it, but she probably would've allowed him to disrobe her and enter her right then if he hadn't been the one to step back and set her primly on her feet as though the kiss had not occurred.

"I'm afraid I can't answer your questions, Emily. If you'd like to stay around for something else, I'm happy to oblige. Otherwise, if you're just here to interrogate, I do have plans."

She glared at him, at least when she finally moved her gaze from his impressive arousal jutting out in front of him. It was a little daunting to think about taking it inside her, but part of her was eager for the challenge.

She tried to quash that part. "I'm not going to give up on this. I know you're up to something, and I'm going to find out what." She poked him in the chest for emphasis.

His hand wrapped around hers, squeezing lightly for a moment, but it was a tender caress, not a punishing hold. "I couldn't imagine being followed by a more beautiful pair of brown eyes." As he spoke, he brought her hand to his mouth to kiss it.

She pulled back her hand, wanting to be repulsed, though she was anything but. "Why don't you just tell me what you're up to? Save us both some time."

He turned away from her, casually strolling across the room and seeming unbothered by his nakedness. He'd certainly made no effort to pick up the towel. He paused at the door to his room and called over his shoulder, "You're welcome to join me for a night out if you have fun in mind. Otherwise, I guess I'll see you as you follow me around."

Emily was annoyed at his response, and his continued blocking of the truth. With a sigh of exasperation, she turned and let herself out of his quarters, storming down the corridor. She tried to ignore the tingling in her lips and the moisture in her core that urged her to return and take what he was offering. Could it be that harmful? It was just a physical fling, wasn't it?

What if he was someone evil, or he had bad intentions for Olympus Station? She'd never forgive herself if she dropped her guard with someone who ended up hurting her friends or the station she considered home. No, she had to resist this unwanted attraction and find out what Anthracite was really doing.

Chapter Three

ANTHRACITE WAS DUE to meet with Timorith in just a few minutes, though he would've gladly postponed the meeting, risking irritating his handler, if Emily had been receptive to sticking around. As it was, he'd been distracted most of his earlier shift, so he had little intel to report to his handler when he met with Timorith at the club a while later.

He would be glad when Timorith returned to their home world of Plexon-II, since he much preferred to deliver his reports through the scrambled electronic station established for him. Unfortunately, his handler had chosen to take a vacation at Olympus Station, which meant he expected reports from Anth in person.

He took his seat at the table, amused to see Timorith engaged in flirtatious play with a male sandosi. The sandosi was quite a bit larger than both diabels, and he had his hand protectively on Timorith's shoulder, rubbing the other man in a soothing fashion. If Anthracite recalled correctly, that had something to do with the sandosi mating routine. If he didn't miss his mark, his handler was going to get lucky.

That could explain why Timorith was so abrupt when he said, "What do you have for me today?"

"Nothing much." Anthracite pushed back a dart of guilt. He'd been distracted and not much of a listener, which was actually his task. Ostensibly, his job was bartender at the Olympus Station promenade bar, but in reality, he was an information officer for his government. He was usually a diligent listener, and he had a flawless memory.

No wonder Timorith seemed so surprised. "You didn't get a thing for me today?"

Most beings liked to talk, especially to a bartender, so Anthracite usually had some kind of information to pass along to his government. Since knowledge was the diabels' primary form of currency, he knew it was vital work.

This day, he'd been too distracted though. He just shook his head. "It was a slow day." In reality, it had been a typical day with the usual amount of traffic, and the bar was always full, as were the nightclubs on the station. Aliens and humans often had different sleeping patterns, so it was rare to find a quiet moment at any of the entertainment establishments or the VR deck.

"How unusual. I guess if there's nothing, I'm done then." Timorith's attention was already returning to the sandosi man beside him.

Anthracite nodded, trying to keep his lips from twitching. "Have a good night, sir. I'll see you when you next debrief me."

Timorith didn't bother to answer aside from a wave, so Anthracite slipped back into the crowd. He had no real plans, other than meeting with Timorith, so he was intending to return to his quarters. He wondered briefly if he could convince Emily to join him, but he was certain that was a no. More likely, he'd just spend a little time fantasizing about her as he brought himself pleasure. That had become the extent of his sex life of late.

It was her fault, of course. He taken one look at Emily Ipsy when she arrived for duty at the station almost a year ago, and he'd lost all interest in any female but her. He'd tried to keep his distance, not wanting to get distracted, but then she started following him. Foolishly, he had hoped for a while that she was genuinely interested in him and was just shy.

Gradually, the truth had dawned on him that there was something more to her following him when it proceeded for days on end that turned to weeks without her ever approaching him. She thought he was up to something, and just because she was right didn't mean it didn't wound him.

He wondered if she would believe his intentions were mostly benign. He certainly wasn't doing anything a million other alien operatives throughout the galaxy weren't doing, whether their species was diabel or not. There were spies in every race, and his specialty was simply information-gathering.

He'd never killed anyone or brought harm to someone, and he'd refuse to do so even if his government directly ordered him to. Would that be enough to satisfy her, or would she insist on knowing every detail of his operation, and why he was on Olympus Station?

He couldn't risk blowing his cover, so he had to quell whatever attraction he felt for her. That's why she'd become practically his nightly companion as he stroked himself while imagining how it would be to take the petite human as his lover.

He was working up quite an erection just thinking about it. The fantasy of what might've happened if he hadn't been a gentleman and stepped back earlier in his quarters had him almost too preoccupied to notice the flash of white ahead of him. Something about it caught his attention though, and his thoughts cleared immediately.

Wings? Was that what he'd seen? He thought it might be. Several species had wings. Some of those had white wings too. With the number of aliens in the galaxies, it would be unusual if there weren't winged extraterrestrials, but something about this particular set put his teeth on edge.

He'd never seen an angrill in the flesh. The war that had raged between the races and decimated great swaths of both their populations had occurred well before his lifetime, but he'd studied enough of his race's history to know what they looked like.

Unable to ignore his curiosity, he followed, turning where he'd seen the flash of white and walking down the corridor. He was looking around, wondering if he'd missed the individual, or if he had simply imagined everything, when he heard a rustling in front of him. He braced himself as he started around the corner, wondering what he would find.

Instead of a white-winged angrill, he ran straight into Emily Ipsy. His arms wrapped around her automatically to hold her against him.

Chapter Four

SHE GLARED UP AT HIM, startled to find herself in his arms. "What are you doing? You're sneaking again?"

He frowned. "Just what are you doing?"

"I was following someone suspicious."

He heaved a sigh. "As I've told you many times, Emily, I mean no harm to anyone. Can't you just let it go?"

She put her hands on her hips. "If you must know, it wasn't you. It was an angrill."

He stiffened. "An angrill?"

She nodded. "They're such an unusual sight that I was curious, so I followed him. I saw him trying to gain access to a supply room, but I think he realized I was following him. I wanted to keep him from knowing for certain, so I had the computer track him while I went through the conduits to catch up with him. I lost the signal about a minute ago, so I climbed out of the conduit and came looking for him. Instead, I found you." She couldn't keep out the note of accusation in her tone.

He glared at her, looking genuinely angry for the first time that she'd known him. It made her shudder a little. "You'd better not be suggesting I'm working with an angrill, Agent Ipsy."

The ice in his tone and the use of her formal title sent a chill down her spine, and she realized she was unhappy that he was angry with her. She shouldn't have such a response when he could very well be a suspect either in whatever was happening, or his own plot. He'd as much admitted he wasn't fully sharing his real reason for being on Olympus Station, so she certainly couldn't trust him. "Why not?"

His scowl darkened. "Surely you must know about the history between his race and mine?"

Emily shrugged a shoulder. "Not really. Your people were at war once, weren't they?"

"A lot more than that." His hand wrapped around her bicep, pulling her along behind him as he marched forward.

She tried to dig in her heels. "Where are you taking me?" Her hand hovered near her comm, but she hesitated to activate it. Perhaps she was being foolish and should act immediately, but still she wavered.

Instead of somewhere nefarious where he could hurt her, he simply chose the nearest public comm room and shoved her inside, entering behind her and locking the door. "Use your authorization code to keep anyone from coming in."

"I will not." She crossed her arms over her chest as she glared at him. "I'm not going to seal off this room so you can murder me in private."

He surprised her by laughing, though there was a hard edge to it. "I'm not going to murder you. I just want to tell you something. I have things I have to do, so you can either accept an explanation or not, but I'm not doing it with the door vulnerable."

After hesitation and sizing him up, she said, "Computer, block this room temporarily. Authorization Tao Beta one-one-four-two."

"Yes, Agent Ipsy," at the computer.

The door flashed green for a moment, indicating the new security protocol was enacted. No one would be able to enter or leave until Emily authorized it, or until someone of higher rank overrode her authorization.

He surprised her by gesturing to one of the chairs. "Have a seat."

She glared at him. "I'd rather stand." It would give her more freedom to move and dart out of his range.

He rolled his eyes as he sat down, making a show of keeping his hands where she could see them. "I'm not going to harm you, Emily. I just wanted to tell you about the history between diabels and angrills. A few centuries ago, there was a bloody war. The angrills had enslaved us, and my people rose up in rebellion. We escaped their worlds and colonies, but they destroyed our home world in retaliation, sending us scattering to the wind and establishing our own colonies anywhere that might keep us from being detected.

"The diabels were even on Earth for a time, until the angrills brought the fight there too. Humans got involved, and we ended up woven into their lore. We left after a time, not wanting to see more innocents injured in the fight between us and the angrills, and we found other places to settle.

"As years passed, a lot of the rancor started to fade as more of our people distanced themselves. The diabels were freed, no longer enslaved by the angrills, and most of us just wanted to live. But there's still animosity, and I guarantee you no angrill and diabel would work together. Do you see how offensive your question is?"

With a sigh, she sat down and nodded as she did so. "I guess. I didn't realize it was still that bad between your peoples. Didn't you almost drive each other to extinction?"

He leaned forward slightly. "For a while, the angrills seemed to have gone extinct. We went several hundred years without seeing a sighting anywhere, but we've noticed a resurgence in the last century or so. They're clearly rebuilding their society and regrouping, but most of them make their living as mercenaries or worse, traversing the galaxies rather than trying to form a cohesive society. It's probably best for diabels and angrills in the long run, since it should prevent renewed hostilities, but we still keep our collective eyes out for them."

Emily let out a sigh of relief. "So that's why you're on Olympus Station? You're here to monitor for the appearance of angrills?"

He hesitated, looking as though he was torn for a moment. Eventually, he shook his head. "The diabels' numbers were severely depleted, as were our resources. We finally managed to scrounge together enough to buy a new planet a few centuries ago, but Plexon-II isn't exactly a wealth of resources. Instead, my people took to exchanging information as a form of trade and currency. You can buy all sorts of things with the right information, including influence, resources, and provisions for one's people. To get that kind of information, we have operatives spread out everywhere, and our jobs are to pay attention. All we do is listen and take notes and pass along that information."

She glared at him. "You're here to spy on all of us?"

He shrugged. "It's my job. It has also allowed me to make some contacts, so I occasionally get things people want, like when the commander's first wife wanted someone to override the block in her biochip program so she could get pregnant. Of course, I assumed it would be with the commander, but I didn't ask. Those are the little things I've done. I guess you could accuse me of some smuggling here and there, but nothing dangerous. I have no interest in hurting anyone. I only trade in information."

She leaned back in her chair, no longer frightened of him, but uncertain how to feel. "You're still spying on people."

He chuckled as he leaned forward, arching a brow at her. "And you aren't?" He looked around for a moment. "With all this technology, I'm certain the computer on the station can tap into anyone's conversation without special equipment. Am I correct?"

Emily shifted slightly in her seat, discomforted by the question. "Yeah, I suppose," she said grudgingly.

"Have you used that information to stop crimes before?"

She frowned. "Of course, we have."

"You've never used it for anything less than life-or-death?"

Emily looked away, recalling Venathi's role at Coalition Headquarters. She herself had never used spying, other than following

Anthracite, but she couldn't pretend it didn't happen. "Okay, I concede your point. So why are you following an angrill? Was it just because you'd seen one, or was there something suspicious about him?"

"There's nothing suspicious for certain, but since you saw him and recognized him as such, I need to talk to my handler."

"How did he disappear though?"

He hesitated as he reached into his pocket, pulling out a device she had never seen. "I suspect he has some kind of stealth technology that he can use to jam signals. He wouldn't wear it all the time, because the computer would notice and investigate a steady jamming signal. He probably only activates it when he's doing something he doesn't want people to know about, or he doesn't want to leave an electronic trail."

She frowned as he opened the device, intrigued by what he was doing while her thoughts also swirled around the angrill's intent. "What might he be doing?"

"If he's working as a mercenary, the question is, what wouldn't he do? Most of them are paid to do what's required, questions unasked. It's part of their code or some nonsense."

There was a beeping sound from his device, and a holographic image of the head of the man she'd seen before appeared on the screen, with a sandosi behind him. From the way they were positioned, it appeared he was sitting on the sandosi's lap.

"What is it, Anthracite?" He sounded impatient and spoke in Diabelish.

Anthracite answered in the same language. "I spotted an angrill on the station, Timorith."

Timorith stood up suddenly, his concern obvious. "You're certain?"

"Very certain. I saw the wings, but we have full identification from a security agent on the station."

Timorith scowled. "Why are you taking a security agent into your confidence?"

"It's all right, Timorith. She's my lover."

Emily gasped, quickly turning it into a cough when Timorith's gaze moved in her direction. She thought about protesting or setting him straight, but she assumed there was a reason Anthracite had made such a bold claim. She wouldn't reveal the lie yet—or that she understood their language.

"I'll see what I can find out about any angrills in the area. Keep your eyes open, Anthracite." With that, Timorith disappeared from the device, and Anth closed it with a click.

He looked at her. "I need to look for him."

"I heard."

He frowned. "What do you mean, you heard?"

Emily grinned. "I'm pretty good with languages, and since I started investigating you, I've been learning Diabelish. You probably know the Coalition database has spotty translation due to some of the similarities in your pronunciations with the tarsas, so I've been studying manually. I'm not completely fluent, but I got the gist of the conversation, I assure you. Why the hell did you tell him I was your lover?"

He put the device in his pocket as he leaned back, looking unconcerned. "There were two reasons."

"What's the first?"

"He won't object nearly so much about your involvement if he believes we're personally connected. I have a feeling I might need your help before this ends, so I wanted to keep that possibility easily open without having to hide it from him."

"I see you're okay hiding everything from me, but not him." As she made the accusation, Emily realized how silly it was. Anthracite barely knew her, and he was clearly at least well-acquainted with his handler if they weren't friends.

He ignored her response. "We might need to work together on this, if you're willing?"

She crossed her arms over her chest. "It depends."

"On what?" He cocked a brow.

"What was your second reason for lying?"

He leaned forward with a slow grin. "Let's just call it wishful thinking, Emily."

Chapter Five

HE SAW HER ALARM, UNDERLAID with a hint of desire, as he uttered the words. He leaned back a little more. "I suggest we go somewhere more secure to discuss our partnership."

She looked skeptical, but she surprised him by nodding and authorizing the computer to unlock the door. He was further surprised when she led him to a lift that was clearly heading toward the crew quarters.

He followed her and was inside her personal quarters moments later. Now that he knew where she lived, he made a note of it, foolishly hoping he might have an invitation to return for more intimate reasons in the future.

She let him in, and he was impressed by the coziness of her quarters. Like most of the crew and residents of Olympus Station, she had made it her own. He walked over to look out the window, noticing she had a view of the port a few decks below. It wasn't exactly prime viewing space, but at least she had a window. He had interior quarters, so he didn't get one.

He turned to her. "Are you going to say anything about what I said?"

She just gave him a look that was difficult to read. "Why do you think you're going to need my help?"

"You have access to the station systems that I don't. I want you to ask the computer to call up the surveillance system to see if there's any video of the angrill."

She hesitated for a moment before walking to her comm station. She sat down, and he took a seat near her, not bothering to wait for an invitation that he had a feeling might never come.

She placed her palm on the scanner, unlocking it biometrically instead of uttering her authorization code, which he knew would be different from the one issued for her security detail. That one was relatively common knowledge but would only be acknowledged by the computer if it recognized her voice and matched her physical characteristics via the security system. The privacy of her personal comm station was less secure, probably due to a desire to balance crew privacy with security.

"Computer, call up footage for me." Emily gave her authorization and specified what data she wanted, and the screen loaded a moment later with visuals of an angrill. Anth's stomach tightened with dread, but that was a purely visceral response perhaps engrained in his DNA.

At first, the angrill was doing nothing untoward, other than walking down the corridor. Video captured him trying to get into the supply room where Emily had first noticed him trying to enter, and then it followed him until he turned the corner. Seconds before Anthracite would've appeared to see him, he flickered out of view. "That's stealth technology," said Anthracite. He'd confirmed his supposition.

"I didn't know that kind of technology could get past our sensors and security system."

He reached out a hand to put on her shoulder since she sounded discouraged. "Unlimited funds and no conscience can produce a great many tools that will surprise you. Hopefully, he has no more in his arsenal."

She frowned. "How does he have unlimited funds if their people are as depleted as yours?"

"Because he works as a mercenary, like most of them. They don't seem to be focused on regrouping a centralized government or coming together as a people. They're ruthless and reckless. Most angrills will take any job that comes along, and that usually pays well. He's a danger to the station, not just to me or other diabels."

Emily looked disturbed, and he wanted to soothe her. Part of him wished he hadn't been so blunt, but he needed her to understand the threat they faced if the angrill was here for some mission. It seemed unlikely he was here just for vacation, though that wasn't an uncommon practice among some beings who lived far out of the major shipping lanes and wanted somewhere to stop for midpoint journeys other places.

No, there was something purposeful about the angrill as he moved in the video, which was looping again, and he watched the angrill's movements analytically, but he was unable to determine much. "We should find out what's in that storage room."

"I also need to modify the computer to look for his stealth technology." She hesitated for a moment before saying, "Computer, call Venathi in her personal quarters."

Anthracite didn't speak as the call went through, wondering who Venathi was. A surge of jealousy went through him as he imagined a handsome human appearing on the screen, one who'd obviously been intimate with *his* Emily. Even knowing she wasn't really his didn't dilute his anger at the thought.

"What do you need?" Instead of a handsome human, it was a faetian who appeared on the screen, her pale green skin, pointed ears, and elfin features finely drawn and eye-catching along with her swath of short blonde hair.

"Do you have access to any special technology?" Emily quickly explained what she needed, and Anthracite tried to ignore Venathi's open curiosity each time she looked at him.

"I think I can rig something for you. I'll send you the schematics as soon as I have it all together." Her attention turned to Anthracite for a moment, their gazes locking. "I guess she ruled you out as a bad guy?"

"That remains to be seen," and Anthracite with a smile.

"I'll get back to you soon." Emily ended connection an instant later

The call had barely ended when Anthracite's comm device beeped, and he pulled it out of his pocket. When he opened it, Timorith's face filled the screen. His friend looked haggard, and Anthracite was sorry he wasn't getting the night he'd probably anticipated spending with the sandosi. "How bad is it?"

"His name is Baatesh Vreesi as far as we can determine. Some of our operatives have tracked him in the past and followed him to a nearby location before losing him."

"He has masking technology. Emily has visual proof of that."

Timorith cursed, and Anth winced as he saw Emily flush slightly. Apparently, her learning of his language included some common swearwords. "And who is Baatesh Vreesi?"

"A nasty piece of work. He's one of the most brutal of the angrills, and from what we can glean, there's no job he won't do. He's even been linked to bombing an orphanage when they refused to sell land a developer wanted on Lotus Twelve."

Emily gasped and stiffened, making him reach out instinctively to take her hand for comfort. "Do we know what he's doing here?"

"We have no notion. I'll let you know soon as I know something, and I'm extending my stay for a while."

Anthracite nodded as the device clicked and Timorith's face disappeared. He looked at Emily, who still held his hand. She was obviously distraught, and he could see her fear. He could practically feel it oozing off her in waves. He squeezed. "We're going to stop him, whatever he's planning."

"I guess we're working together then." Her expression turned stern. "You'd better not betray me or pull any spy crap on me. We have total truthfulness between us while working together. Agreed?"

He nodded. "I agree with that. For what it's worth, I don't like keeping secrets, though it's a necessary part of my job sometimes."

"Your job seems to be all about sharing secrets," she said tartly.

"I suppose I can see why you'd say that. Let me specify that when it comes to my personal life with friends and lovers, I don't keep secrets if I can help it at all. Are we clear?"

She tugged her hand away. "That hardly matters, Anthracite. We're simply working together to find out what Baatesh is doing. I suggest we come up with a schedule so we can coordinate our efforts. Once Venathi sends the technology, we'll have a way to track him."

He bit down his disappointment, not arguing with her. She seemed not to want to be involved with him, but her body sent an entirely different message every time they touched. He could've taken her against the door earlier if he had been less honorable and also hadn't feared consequences of her having second thoughts and regrets afterward.

He hadn't wanted that to happen. If and when she came to his bed, he wanted it to be completely willingly, with her full consent, awareness, and participation. "I think that's a good idea." With that, he tried to shove aside his personal feelings and his attraction to Emily so they could focus on the business at hand.

If they couldn't discover what Baatesh's mission was and stop it, there was a strong possibility there'd be no chance for any kind of future between them anyway. A man who could blow up an orphanage would do all manners of atrocities, and he was determined to protect Emily and Olympus Station from that.

Chapter Six

AS PROMISED, VENATHI had sent the schematics and the program within two days, which allowed her to track Baatesh wherever he might be on Olympus Station even when he engaged his masking technology. She'd met with Anthracite long enough to give him a copy of the technology as well, wondering if she should turn it over to the commander instead as she surrendered a copy to him.

Was she betraying her people and her station by working with the diabel? She had no answer, but he seemed as sincerely interested in investigating Baatesh as she was.

A couple of days after that, she found herself trailing the inscrutable angrill since it was her turn. There was no discernible pattern to his route, which made it harder to track him. Why was he entering this section of the station? It wasn't entirely off-limits to non-crewmembers, but there was little reason he'd have to be in the reactor area unless he was visiting someone there.

Not knowing his intentions was solely why she didn't involve her partner and call for backup or escalate the situation. There was so much to explain that she was hesitant to do so until she had firmer proof of wrongdoing.

She followed behind him, looking down at the small device attached to her wrist comm. The shrill beeping clued her in that it wasn't working any longer. She paused and tapped it with her finger, wondering what was wrong with it.

She looked around, trying to establish visual contact without getting too close. Why was her technology no longer working?

The answer dawned on her even as he stepped into view. This was a shielded area, meant to block out high radiation, and it likely blocked out the signal since it was coming from her device rather than amplified through the security system itself and transmitted to her device.

As she had the realization, he appeared before her. Her first thought was he was absolutely beautiful. The angrill standing before her had silvery skin, long white hair that flowed down his back, and magnificent plumage from his wings that stretched out on either side of him to full capacity, filling the space of the corridor and blocking her way forward. His eyes were as monochromatic as the rest of him, with white sclera and silver pupils and irises, and his face was perfection.

Icy perfection that revealed nothing, yet still sent a shiver of dread up her spine.

"Why are you following me?" His gravelly voice was a marked contrast to the beautiful exterior. She'd expected his speech to sound like music playing judging from his physical beauty, rather than the gruff, slightly astringent note.

She shook her head. "I don't know what you're talking about."

His wings ruffled slightly, and he crossed his arms over his chest as he gave her a stern look. "Don't try my intelligence, human. You've clearly been following me for a while, so explain yourself."

She crossed her arms over her chest before thinking better of it and dropping one hand to her side, so she could grasp her taser if needed. Why hadn't she packed her pistol instead? "I don't know what you're accusing me of, but I've done nothing wrong. I'm a security agent on Olympus Station. What are you doing here?" She waved her hand. "You have no legitimate reason to be in this area."

His lips twitched, though it was like marble moving. "I don't need to explain myself to you, human." The level of condescension in his tone was irritating.

"You do if I request it. I'm authorized to act to maintain the safety of the station. I want an explanation for your actions, including what you're doing in this area and on Olympus Station."

"I'm still disinclined to share such information with you." He started to turn away from her, his wings ruffling the air around them and sending a breeze her direction.

Emily reached for her taser. "Stop right there. You're under arrest."

He turned so quickly that she hadn't expected him to move that fast. She hadn't been that close to him, but he closed the gap in under a second, one of his wings beating against her with enough force to send her flying. She collided with the rail and clung to it, suddenly and grimly reminded of how Baxter Frink's body had looked after he took a similar plunge months before while trying to kill the commander's now-wife.

He stared at her for a moment, appearing completely at ease when he uttered a threat. "Stay away, human, if you know what's good for you." With those words, he spun on his heel, hopped to the top of the railing, and jumped. She cried out in shock though wasn't surprised when his wings flapped, and he started flying away, gradually descending as he did so.

Emily was shaken by the encounter, and her ribs hurt. She'd bitten her lip when she slammed into the rail, and the wise thing to do would be to visit Dr. Gretel, but she didn't want to explain her injuries.

She needed some help healing her ribs though. She had a marked lack of allies at the moment, with Anthracite being the only one who knew she'd been following the angrill.

With a grimace of pain, she got to her feet, hugging her arms around her ribs. She took slow, shallow breaths that caused great pain with each inhalation and exhalation.

It was slow going, but she finally arrived at Anthracite's quarters twenty minutes later, having to move deliberately while trying to appear inobtrusive and hide her injuries. She collapsed against his door after pressing the ringer, suddenly worried he wouldn't be home.

The door opened a moment later, and she fell inward as he caught her in his arms. She clung to him, somehow managing to stay upright when he pulled her inside. The door closed behind them, and she started to sag against it, but he wouldn't let go.

"What happened to you?" As he asked, he was visually inspecting her, and his hands started to glide over her body in an assessing fashion. Even in her pain, his touch caused a frisson of awareness to shoot through her.

"Baatesh caught me following him. He wanted an explanation I refused to provide, so he assaulted me."

The change in Anthracite's demeanor was instant and obvious. He went from concerned to enraged, and his tail started jerking furiously. "How dare he put his hands on you? I'll kill him."

"Maybe later," she said with a hint of amusement. "Right now, I could use your help with a regenerator. I'm afraid I can't get the correct angle."

He scowled. "You should go to the Med Bay."

Emily frantically shook her head. "I can't do that. I'll have to explain what happened if I do, and I don't have enough evidence yet to bring this to the commander."

He frowned as he picked her up, ignoring her protests, though she wasn't really objecting that hard. It was strange to be carried by a man, but there was something soothing and protective about the motion as well. All too soon, he placed her on the couch, arranging her so she could lie flat with her injured side exposed to him.

"I doubt you would get in trouble for noticing he's skulking around and is clearly a threat." As he spoke, Anthracite's fingers deftly dealt with the shirt of her uniform, pulling it from the waistband of her pants and tucking it up until it was just under her breasts. She shivered as one of his fingers lightly skimmed her abdomen, though she thought it was by accident.

"I prefer to have solid proof before I go to him." She was embarrassed to admit how far her ambition had driven her outside the parameters of her job description. She was overzealous at best, and Commander Templeton might even interpret it as insubordination or going against orders if she explained her activities of the past few weeks and how she'd initially become suspicious of Baatesh.

Part of her reticence was also reluctance to implicate Anthracite in the situation, since the commander was bound to have questions for him if he learned Emily had been following the bartender, acting on suspicions on her own. It was an uneasy place to be, torn between loyalties, and knowing she'd brought it on herself did little to assuage her guilt or clarify a path forward.

"I suppose I can take care of this, but if the scanner shows anything beyond my capability, I'm taking you straight to Med Bay. Deal?"

Emily nodded as he moved away from her, disappearing from her sight for a moment. When he returned, he held a med scanner in his left hand, and a cell regenerator in his right.

He knelt on the floor and scanned her abdomen and ribs, frowning at the results, though he didn't look too concerned. "The bastard broke three of your ribs."

"Do I have any internal bleeding?" It was difficult to speak since it was hard to draw in a deep breath. She trembled from the exertion.

"No. The regenerator should see to your needs." He set aside the scanner and shifted the regenerator, slowly pressing the probe against her broken ribs. Emily cried out at the agony of contact, understanding he had to apply enough pressure to allow the bones to knit together with the help of the accelerated healing process, but it was still five minutes of agony.

Slowly, her breathing returned to normal, and the pain lessoned before disappearing. Then she was aware of the throbbing in her lip where she'd bitten it, but she didn't have to mention that to Anthracite. After using the scanner once more and nodding in satisfaction, which nonverbally confirmed the regenerator had done its job—Emily had already realized that due to the loss of pain—he brought the regenerator to her mouth, gently passing it over her sensitive lip and the cut inside.

It took far less time to heal, and she felt pain-free seconds later, though severe exhaustion was taking over. That was a side effect of using the accelerator, since it required so much energy to quickly produce the cells hastened by the process.

"Stay with me long enough to get you some food, Emily. Then you can sleep for a while." He got to his feet. "What should I synthicate for you?"

She mumbled something, not even sure herself what she said. Her eyes tried to close, but she turned her head to follow him with her gaze, though she could barely keep her eyes open.

Anth returned a few moments later with some sort of broth. It didn't taste familiar, so she wondered if it was a diabel dish as she did her best to drink it. He held the bowl for her while supporting her head with his other hand. She managed a few sips before lifting a hand to wave it away. "No more." Her voice was slurred, and she slumped against his arm, no longer able to hold herself up.

"I wish you'd eat more." He sounded exasperated as he set it aside. "You seem too out of it though."

Emily didn't bother to confirm his supposition. She was simply too exhausted to keep her eyes open, and they drafted closed a moment later.

EMILY WOKE SOMETIME later, feeling disoriented for a moment before she remembered where she was. She felt much better now that she was well rested. She looked around as she sat up, startled to see Anthracite dozing in the armchair nearby. She was surprised he'd sat vigil with her, though she supposed she shouldn't be. He was a bit shady sometimes, but he was clearly a good person, and there was obviously a connection between them.

She started to sit up fully, swinging her feet off the couch and onto the floor so she could stand up. Her plan was to leave him sleeping so he could get some rest without her disturbing him, but as she started to walk past him, his tail snaked out and snagged her around the waist, pulling her down onto his lap. She squealed in shock even as she braced herself against him and then clung to him for a moment. "What are you doing?"

His eyes opened, and he flashed her a lazy grin. "I just wanted to check on you."

She ran her hand pointedly down his tail, which made his eyes drooped for a moment, and he shivered. She couldn't help wondering if it was an erogenous zone, which should have made her hand pull away instead of wrapping more firmly around the length of the appendage. "You could just ask."

His eyes opened again, but there was still an air of laziness about him. No, more unhurried than lazy. "Where's the fun in that, Emily?"

"I'm fine. Thanks for your help, Anthracite."

"So formal." His tone was teasing as his hand grasped her chin, ensuring she continued to look at him. "Are you leaving?"

She looked pointedly down at his tail again, once more squeezing the circumference and getting a small purr from him for her trouble. "I plan to."

"Maybe you should stay in case you have a relapse."

She shivered as his chest rumbled when he spoke, making her body vibrate. "I'm sure I'll be fine." There was a marked lack of conviction in her words though. Of course, she didn't have to worry about a relapse. The technology had healed her, accelerating her own response by stimulating her immune system, but the lack of conviction came from waffling about whether she really wanted to leave.

The truth was, she didn't. When he bent his head to kiss her, it felt inevitable, and she lifted her mouth to meet has. The kiss they exchanged was like lighting a match that quickly consumed them both in a blazing inferno of desire. He stood up, clutching her to him before slinging her over his shoulder in a not-so-sexy move that made her giggle.

Her head spun as blood rushed to her brain. Emily giggled and shrieked, trying to escape his firm clutches as he strode through his quarters. From her vantage point, she could see the dimples in the metal floor and the way the synthetic fabric clung to his shapely buttocks. Her gaze focused there, and her panties were soaked by the time he dropped her gently onto his bed.

Sprawling there, and making no move to put her legs together, she grinned up at him. "There's room for two, Anth."

He laughed. "Good, because we're going to need every inch so I can do all the wicked things playing through my mind."

She licked her lips. "That sounds naughty." Patting the bed beside her, she said, "Tell me more."

"I'd rather show you." He stripped off his black Olympus Station bar uniform shirt in a fluid motion. "I prefer a hands-on style of instruction." His shoes and socks went next.

"Nice." Emily kicked off her shoes. "I'm a fast learner, Anth."

"It's okay if you aren't." He removed his pants, shucking them off quickly. His briefs joined the pile of his clothing. "I don't mind showing you as many times as it takes. Night after night, until we reach a mutually satisfactory understanding."

He dropped onto the bed beside her, his mouth seeking out hers. Emily surrendered to the kiss even as little alarm bells rang in the back of her mind. Part of her wanted to break away to make sure he understood this was just physical. One night only. She didn't want anything more serious with someone she didn't know she could trust. Did she?

Deciding it was meaningless flirtation, and setting boundaries was unnecessary, she let herself enjoy his mouth on hers. Anth was probably good at the one-night thing and had his whole routine down. He was just saying what he thought she wanted to hear by implying he wanted more than just a quick fuck. She wanted more than a quick fuck too, but nothing approaching a relationship or commitment. She wanted to focus on her career and be promoted, not get distracted by love. Right?

Anth kissed his way down her neck as his hand slipped under the waistband of her pants. Emily lifted her bottom to help him slide them down, scooting into a semi-seated position to roll them off her body. With an enthusiastic fling, she tossed them toward his pile of clothes. Her shirt followed a moment later.

He wasted no time in stripping off the red bra to reveal her full breasts, which she'd always considered too large for her frame. He didn't seem to mind the generosity of her globes. Cradling each one in his hands, he thumbed her nipples as he bent his head to kiss her again. She curled nearer to him, plundering his mouth with her tongue as Anth caressed her breasts.

He broke the kiss to move his head downward, taking one of her nipples between his lips. The contrast of her lighter skin against his red shade was beautiful and only fueled her arousal. She had never been with an alien before, but it wasn't because she had a hang-up about it. With her limited time and focus on career first, she'd hardly been with any men, regardless of species.

Anth slowly pulled away from her breast, taking a moment to run his black tongue around the hardened pebble before speaking. "God, you're beautiful, Emily. Just perfection."

Her face flamed with color at the extravagant comment. "I'm already in your bed, so you don't have to lay it on so thick," she teased.

He nodded, looking earnest. "I'm grateful, but I'm not feeding you a line. I love your body. Full breasts and rounded hips..." Trailing off, he cupped her hips, lifting her effortlessly to sit on his stomach as he laid on his back. His hands slipped lower to cup her butt. "Lush ass."

Grinding her hips so that her slippery folds pressed against the muscles of his abdomen, she said, "Wet pussy."

Anth groaned, seeming to lose all vestiges of control. One hand remained on her buttocks, but the other moved around and between their bodies. Wriggling into the tight space between them, his fingers brushed her clit as he stroked her moist slit. "You aren't lying."

"I never lie." Emily arched against his hand as he tested her moisture by thrusting two fingers inside her. It had been a while since she'd had a real cock in there, and she winced just a bit but also enjoyed the stretching sensation. Knowing how well-endowed he was, she appreciated his preparation.

Anth hesitated for a second, pressing against her clitoris without moving.

Annoyed by his teasing, she rocked against him. "Touch me, *shogash*." She hoped she had nailed the proper pronunciation of the word that roughly translated as sweetheart or lover.

With another loud groan, he circled her clit with his thumb while his fingers continued to surge inside her. Emily rode his hand as she wanted to ride him. Already, his fingers weren't enough, since her sheath had adjusted to the invasion. "Please, Anth, fuck me."

"Emily." His movements were jerky as he slid her lower, bringing the head of his cock to nestle against her folds. He was as thick and big as she remembered. His smooth shaft lacked a head like human males, but it had a rounded tip that helped as he started guiding it inside her.

Emily rocked against him, moaning as he slipped inside her, stretching her in a deliciously familiar way that she had almost forgotten existed. It hurt for a moment, but once he was fully inside, that flash of discomfort faded. "So good," she whispered, unable to form complete sentences and afraid to speak too loudly lest she give in to the screams of pleasure building in her chest. She was not going to be a screamer.

Anth slowly filled her, surging up into her until she was snug around him. Emily clenched her inner muscles, making him moan. He began to thrust harder and faster, and she met each motion of his body. Their coupling was fast, but satisfying, speaking to her on a primal level.

As his cock dragged against her g-spot, she hovered on the edge of orgasm. With a cry and contractions deep in her womb, she surrendered to bliss. Her body spasmed around his hardening cock, and she almost clamped her thighs around him to keep Anth inside her as he pushed deeper into her. She was beyond being mortified by the small scream of pleasure that escaped her.

The hot splash of Anth's satisfaction hit her insides a second later. Two more pulses followed the first before he sighed and relaxed. Anth laid back, drawing her against him so she curled next to him.

He brushed a soft kiss against her temple, and she thought about saying something but was too languorous to summon the effort. In a euphoric cloud of post-coital satisfaction, she let her eyes close and rested against her lover, deciding she could spare a few minutes to enjoy the moment before they began their pursuit of Baatesh once more.

Chapter Seven

IT WASN'T ENTIRELY surprising that Emily had fallen into another deep sleep after their passionate lovemaking. Healing the body so rapidly took a lot out of it, and he watched over her for a while, content to hold her in his arms. Yet the more he thought about Baatesh attacking her, the angrier he grew.

Compelled to do something about it, he gently moved away from her, carefully leaving her to sleep in his bed with her head on his pillow. It was a pleasant thought to know it would smell like her upon his return, though he hoped she would still be there waiting for him. If he was swift about his mission, he could return before she even knew he was gone.

He dressed quickly, donning his wrist comm and pulling up the tracking technology integrated with his system, provided by Emily's friend. He immediately found Baatesh's signal, and he frowned when he realized the other man was in the storage areas once again. That had been where Emily had seen him before, trying to access a room for which he had no authority to be in.

Anthracite had no weapon, but he could take comfort in knowing Baatesh likely didn't have one either. He had stealth technology, but it was still difficult to smuggle in a weapon with the security protocols in place on Olympus Station. Anyone who came armed to the station had to surrender their weapons during their stay, or else they had to leave them on their ship.

He wasn't certain whether Baatesh had surrendered or merely stowed them on his ship, but he felt reasonably secure as he approached the location from where he was picking up the signal minutes later. Baatesh had not moved, and he was clearly trying to get into something. Anthracite approached as quietly as possible, freezing for a moment at the sight of the angrill moving furtively, his wings hiding his activities, though it appeared he was trying to gain access to a storage room.

Anger overtook Anthracite, shoving aside any sense of caution, and he sped forward, plowing into the angrill and knocking him into the wall opposite the door. He pinned his arm against Baatesh's throat, barely resisting the urge to press harder than he needed to keep the other man still. "You keep your hands off Emily."

"Friend of yours?" The angrill's voice was rough, and he seemed to have difficulty speaking, but Anthracite didn't loosen his hold. "You should tell your little human not to follow me if she wants to avoid injury."

"What are you doing on Olympus Station?"

Baatesh's face revealed nothing. It was just cold perfection, and he could see why angrills had inspired some of the greatest sculptors in multiple aliens' history. They were beautiful on the exterior, though most of them were rotten to the core.

"That's my business and only my business, diabel." With a grunt, Baatesh shoved them forward, using his wings as a springboard. Anth's back slammed into the corridor behind him, sending a jolt of pain through him.

He gritted his teeth to absorb it, maintaining his grasp on Baatesh so the other man didn't get the upper hand. "Get you and your things off Olympus Station."

"It's an unrestricted zone for Coalition members, and angrills are Coalition members."

"Barely. You don't even have an organized civilization. Your home world is in shambles."

Baatesh's eyes flickered, which looked like little flashes of lightning in his irises. "At least our home world remains intact. We didn't have to find a new one that's third-rate at best." The angrill chuckled, clearly satisfied with himself.

"Don't push me, angrill. I want you gone from Olympus Station in the next hour."

"Or what?" With a cold laugh, Baatesh suddenly punched him in the solar plexus. Try as he did, Anthracite was not able to absorb the painful blow without flinching and falling to his knees, inadvertently releasing his hold on Baatesh. "Stay out of my way if you want to live, diabel."

With those words, Baatesh darted around the corner and disappeared from sight. Anthracite would've followed him, but it took several moments to regain his breath and the ability to stand. He wasn't going to need cell regeneration, but he definitely needed time to recuperate.

Once he could walk again without betraying any obvious signs of pain, he returned to his quarters, going a little slower than he had left them. When he entered the room, he found Emily standing close to the door, clearly waiting for him.

She wore only his pajama shirt, and it was the sexiest thing he'd ever seen. Temporarily forgetting about his injury and the confrontation with Baatesh, he grasped a handful of the front of the shirt and pulled her toward him, his mouth descending to kiss her.

She put quietus to that by placing her hand between them, making his lips brush against her fingers instead. "Where were you?"

With a sigh, he released her. "I was confronting Baatesh."

She frowned. "That was dangerous. You should've woken me so I could go with you."

"I don't know what he's up to, but he was trying to get into that storage room again. I suggest we see what's in there." He ignored her admonishment to involve her in the situation. He wanted to protect her as much as possible, even though he knew that wasn't entirely possible given her job and her involvement in the situation.

She sighed, clearly annoyed with him, though she didn't pursue it. "Give me a few minutes to get dressed."

He was tempted to suggest they check out the room another time, but he restrained himself. The task before them was too important to be forgotten or pushed aside, even by the most amazing sex of his life.

Moments later, they returned to the storage room, and Emily used her authorization to enter. He looked around, following her, but there was nothing obviously of interest. "It's just a bunch of chemicals and some metals used for repairs around or on the station." Emily shrugged. "I'm not sure why he wants to get in here... Could he be trying to repair his ship without anyone knowing there's something wrong with it?"

He hesitated and then shrugged. "I suppose if he didn't want to go on record as being on Olympus Station for repairs, though it seems unlikely."

Emily nodded, clearly realizing it was a weak theory at best, but it was better than no idea at all. "We just need to keep as close an eye on him as we have been."

He frowned. "I don't want you following him anymore, Emily. He's dangerous."

She put her hands on her hips, clearly gearing up for a fight. "That's my job, and I'm well-trained. I assure you I can handle myself."

He looked pointedly at her side. "Really?"

Her eyes narrowed. "He caught me by surprise. It was an ambush, but he won't do it again. I'll steer clear of any shielded areas that might help him dampen his signal, and I'll hang back. If I see him doing something nefarious, I'll involve you if there's time."

With a growl, he moved forward, grasping her chin to ensure she met his gaze. "No if there's time nonsense. If you think you're going to be confronting him, you call me. We're in this together, Emily."

Her eyes widened with surprise, but she didn't move away. "Really?"

He nodded, unwavering. "I feel like we've been in this together from the beginning. You must know how I feel about you, Emily. I have ever since I first laid eyes on you."

Her eyes widened, and she seemed shocked. "I thought this was just physical?"

He tried to hide how much that injured him. "It isn't for me. It could be just physical for you though."

Her gaze softened, making him suspect he hadn't done that great of a job of hiding his vulnerability. She lifted a hand to cup his cheek. The other one rose a moment later, so she was holding his face in her hands. She looked earnestly at him, and he could see there was more than physical attraction involved. She was clearly engaged emotionally as well. "I told myself it was, even while we were making love, but it's not just physical for me either. When this is over..." She trailed off.

"We'll talk then." He finished the thought by kissing her, and she kissed back. It was nearly an hour later before they left the storage room, having found no clues about why Baatesh had wanted to enter it, but certainly leaving far more satisfied than when they had arrived.

It was difficult to bid goodbye to her outside her quarters, but she didn't invite him in. He knew she had an early shift, so he tried not to take it personally. After the hour they'd spent together, combined with their earlier experience, he was reasonably secure she was being truthful. Emily seemed to feel as much for him as he felt for her, and he looked forward to resolving the situation with Baatesh so he could focus purely on his determined little security agent.

Chapter Eight

AFTER SLEEPING SO MUCH for her recovery, Emily had a difficult time falling back to sleep, so she rose early and got to work before she was scheduled. She waited in the breakroom for Gordon to clock in, and the irascible older man joined her seconds before their shift was due to begin. Since he was on time, she had no reason to be critical or complain, so she kept her irritation to herself. It wasn't Gordon's fault she hadn't slept well and had been up so early.

The day was reasonably routine, at least to start with. Nothing of note happened until midmorning when they were called to the foundry. She and Gordon entered the room, which was hotter than most environments on the station. Even with excellent environmental controls, it was a heated working environment, since it was difficult to regulate. The kilns had to be hot enough to melt the metal, and she started to perspire lightly less than a minute after entering.

Henry James, the supervisor of the section, greeted them. "Thanks for coming."

"You mentioned something about a theft?" Gordon had started recording the interview with his wrist comm, so Emily didn't bother.

"Yeah. We didn't notice to start with, since it's a reasonably small quantity, on a comparative basis, but one of our employees observed the load we're about to ship was two-point-four kilos light."

"Light on what?" asked Gordon before Emily could.

"There were several items. It's a building project for one of the colony planets, so there was copper, steel, and tolalium."

"What is tolalium?" asked Emily.

"From the Tol race. They introduced it as part of their application to the Coalition. It's a flexible metal. Heat easily changes its properties, but it doesn't melt. It retains amazing strength despite being flexible. It's pretty common in construction since it can be molded into just about any shape."

"Is there anybody working for you who'd have reason to take it?" asked Gordon.

Henry shook his head. "I can't think of any reason why any of us would need it. None of us are building anything. I really don't think it was my people, and we have pretty tight security around here."

"We'll make a note and keep an eye out for it. Be sure to report it on your daily incident report," said Emily as she logged the events into her own report.

"Will do. I wanted to get it officially on record. We have enough supplies on hand to finish out the load, so if it's all right, I'll ship it?"

"Let us take a quick look around to make sure there's no evidence left behind, but then you can send it." Gordon stopped recording the interview.

Emily followed behind him as he looked around the load, which was on a maglev skid. Whoever had noticed the theft must have sharp eyes, because it looked like a complete load to her. She assumed there was a system of weighing involved, and the computer had obviously helped with the inventory.

It seemed like an inexplicable and fairly benign crime, though she and Gordon took it seriously. Sometimes, there was a hotbed of criminal activity occurring on the station, and there was likely a black market trade which they haven't traced yet, but there was no proof linking this to any suggestion of a black market or other reasons for theft. It was a mystery.

They were just wrapping up when Emily intercepted a call from the computer when it pinged her. "Yes, Computer?"

"The chemistry department is requesting a security check," said the computer.

Emily made a note of it, looking to Gordon to ensure he'd heard the report. He nodded at her, and they left the foundry moments later to head across the station to the chemistry department.

They entered the section a few seconds after that, and a frantic-looking man with large eyes behind thick glasses approached them. The glasses must be a fashionable affectation, because he could've easily had his vision repaired with modern technology. "It's about time you arrived."

"Why do you need a security check?" asked Emily.

At the same time, Gordon asked, "Who are you, pal?"

"Chester Higgins, and I'm the head chemist. We need you because we've had a theft."

Emily started to feel uneasy. "What kind of theft?"

"Someone has taken a quantity of magnesium, phosphorus, and belenite."

"Who would do that?" asked Gordon. "What would be the purpose?"

The chemist shrugged. "I couldn't explain that. There's no obvious connection, yet we're missing quantities of each. The computer alerted us to the discrepancy just a few minutes ago." As he spoke, he passed over a chip in a clear case. "Here's the report."

"What are the uses for the chemicals?" Emily took the case and tucked it into her pocket as she asked.

Higgins frowned. "I guess it depends on what your aims are. There are reasons I couldn't possibly begin to explain to you, but I can't think of any obvious need for all three. There's not any commonly used formula that combines them."

"What's the belenige stuff?" Gordon looked up from making a note on his wrist comm.

"Belenite," corrected Chester in a demeaning way. "It's simply an enhancer. Its core function is usually to make other chemicals work better."

"Thanks," said Emily. She was recording the interview this time, and she added a few notes. "Let's take a look where the theft occurred."

Chester brought them into a side room filled with supplies. There were liquids and powders lining the shelf, some only half-filled or nearly empty, which made it difficult to identify the specific areas missing inventory. He left them a moment later, clearly far too preoccupied with his important work to watch them document the evidence.

Not that there was any. If it hadn't been for the computer alerting the chemists to the discrepancy in amounts, it would've been difficult to tell there was any theft. With most items in the supply cabinet at least half-depleted, nothing stood out as unusual or missing.

"I'm stymied." Emily made a note of that in her report.

"We've logged the geek's report, so let's get out of here. I could go for some lunch."

Emily nodded, feeling hungry herself, though her mind was still preoccupied with the two reports of theft.

They left the chemistry section but hadn't gone far before the computer chimed to catch their attention. Gordon answered the call this time, quickly ascertaining they were wanted in aquaponics.

Piper Templeton greeted them when they arrived in aquaponics. She was very pregnant, and Emily had sympathy for the poor woman. It must be difficult to have instantly become pregnant when she acted as surrogate for her deceased sister and the commander, but she seemed to have taken to it well. Though she looked a little tired, she was moving with undeniable energy as they approached.

Piper smiled at her and nodded to Gordon, whose expression remained as sour as ever. Emily was certain he didn't dislike Mrs. Templeton. He was just normally a grouch.

"Thank you for coming. The computer alerted me we've had—"

"A theft?" asked Emily.

Piper frowned, but she nodded. "Yes, precisely. We're missing a few kilos of fertilizer. I don't know why anybody would want it besides us, unless they're having trouble with plants in their quarters." She laughed, clearly dismissing the notion. "They could just acquire that through any of the supply masters or the stores on the promenade. I really can't tell why anyone would want fertilizer, but I need to report the theft."

"We'll make a note of it." Emily did so as she spoke. "May we see the area from where it was stolen?"

"Of course." Mrs. Templeton led them into a storage room, which was in a similar situation the other thefts of the morning. It wouldn't have been obvious if the computer hadn't been tracking inventory and realized there was a discrepancy. There was little to be gleaned from the crime scene, and they were departing aquaponics a few moments later.

"I'm heading to lunch."

Emily frowned. "You can't go to lunch yet. We need to figure out why someone has stolen these items from three different sections."

Gordon snorted. "You really think they're connected, do you?"

She put her hands on her hips as she gave him a look of disbelief. "You think it's a coincidence and unconnected that we've had three thefts in the same day?"

He shrugged a shoulder. "Probably just teenagers. Kids trying to outdo each other with pranks. Remember when that group from the school thought it would be hilarious to put Grambian slugs in all the corners of the station they could get to? It took weeks to get rid of the stench."

Emily scowled. "That was a silly prank, but it was benign. They didn't steal anything."

He shrugged. "So they've escalated. I'm not gonna waste my lunch hour worrying about it. You coming along?"

After a moment, she shook her head. "No, I have something else to take care of."

He shrugged a shoulder. "Suit yourself. See after lunch, kid."

Emily rolled her eyes at the paternal diminutive but let it slide. Hayes was a man from a different century, and he thought he knew everything there was to know. She couldn't believe he wasn't treating this as a series of connected thefts.

Annoyed with him, she went to Anthracite's quarters, but he wasn't in. Her next stop was the bar, and she was relieved to see him behind the counter. He was busy though, so she took a seat at the end of the bar, ordering food from the server as she waited for Anthracite to be free.

He managed to get to her a few minutes later, his hand grazing hers where it rested on the countertop. "Can I get you a drink?"

"I have to go back on duty, so no."

He frowned. "You seem upset. What's wrong?" His expression darkened as he scowled. "Has Baatesh come after you again?"

Emily shook her head. "Nothing like that. There's been a series of thefts this morning, and Gordon is as blind as ever, insisting it's all unrelated or just pranks by kids. I'm convinced it's the work of the same person, but I can't see a connection."

"Give me a minute." He was called away by a patron requesting a new drink. She watched him make it quickly and skillfully, impressed by how efficient he was, and how nimble his gorgeous fingers were as he fashioned the Florfial firewheel. He passed it over to the pink alien before returning to her. "What was stolen?"

Emily quickly called up a list and turned her wrist comm to project it for him as a 3-D image.

He stared at it for a moment, clearly reading it once and then rereading it. His brow furrowed, and he looked concerned, but he was flagged down by another patron. He put up a finger in her direction before moving over to help the man waiting, serving his drink quickly.

Emily watched him do it, noticing when he abruptly froze, and there was a new air of anxiety when he returned to her. "Those ingredients can be combined to make a bomb."

A chill of dread spread through her, and her stomach churned with nausea even as she shook her head. "No, that's impossible."

He tilted his head. "Look it up for yourself if you don't believe me, but I'm sure all of those items can be combined to create an IED. You certainly can't smuggle one past Olympus Station security, so if you wanted to bomb something, you'd have to build your own from supplies available once you arrived."

Following a hunch, she pulled up the inventory list for the supply room she'd caught Baatesh trying to get into. Dread curled in her stomach when she noted it held all the supplies that had been stolen from the various departments. Emily's unease turned to outright fear, and she could no longer hold back reporting this. "I have to speak to the commander."

"I'll come with you." As he spoke, he took off his apron and tossed it in the direction of the counter. When the server came by, he said, "Dahzhe, I need you to take over tending bar."

The woman looked shocked. "I don't know how to make the drinks."

"You'll have to muddle through until someone comes to relieve you." Anthracite brooked no room for argument, grasping Emily's hand as he came around the bar to her side and pulled her off the stool, almost dragging her behind him.

When they entered the corridor of thep, she said, "Computer, locate Commander Templeton."

"The commander is in the command module, Agent Ipsy."

She started to head that way, and as she did, Anthracite used his wrist come to pull up Baatesh's signal. He scowled. "It's intermittent. He's found some way to interfere with the technology, but I think I've got it homing in on the sector he's in. He appears to be in crew quarters."

She frowned. "Olympus Station crew quarters, or merchant crew quarters?"

"Olympus Station quarters. I can't get a fix on exactly where he is, but it's in that direction."

Emily was torn, wanting to alert the commander, but also afraid if Baatesh should manage to find a way around their tracking technology, he could plant the bomb before they had a chance to stop him, and t could go off before they discovered its location. "We should go find him."

Anthracite nodded, and Emily was glad she'd brought her laser pistol instead of her taser today. It gave some comfort to her as they turned away from the direction of the command module to head toward the executive crew quarters instead. As they ran, Emily used her wrist comm to contact the commander.

Captain Hadley Wells's face appeared instead of Templeton's on her wrist comm. "What is it, Agent Ipsy?"

"Ma'am, we suspect there's a bomb being placed somewhere in the executive crew quarters. Anthracite and I are heading that way, but we need backup."

"A bomb? What're you talking about?" Hadley looked alarmed, but not alarmed enough. She was still obviously more curious than anything.

"I'll explain it all later, but we need help now." Emily ended the connection, deciding not to waste time trying to persuade Hadley of the incidents that had been happening. There would be time for that later.

They reached the crew quarters moments later, though the technology they'd both used from Venathi was no more precise than it had been even at closer range. They were able to narrow it down to which corridor he was in, but beyond that, they were going to have to search every room.

Emily started using her authorization code to override each door, and they had checked four quarters before they hesitated outside quarters Hadley shared with Nykal, her Jrojan fiancé.

Anthracite stiffened. "Do you hear that?"

She shrugs. "What am I listening for?"

"There's a rustling sound."

Emily couldn't hear it, so it must be outside the range of human hearing, but she was confident in Anthracite's physical abilities. She entered her authorization code, and the door opened a second later. She was certain Hadley was tracking her wrist comm coordinates, and she had no need to contact the commander to let her know where they were. Instead, she quickly tapped an SOS to send silently, not wanting to alert Baatesh to their presence before she had to.

They slipped in quietly, and he apparently hadn't heard the door open. Together, they searched the open living space without seeing any sign of him. Anthracite jerked his head to the left, indicating the corridor down which they would find the bedroom and bathroom, and they headed that way.

The bedroom door was closed, but Emily overrode it by manually typing in her authorization code. When it opened with a hydraulic kiss, she went in first, gun drawn. Anthracite was right behind her, and she appreciated him letting her take lead without trying to make a macho deal out of it since she was the one who was armed.

"Freeze." She issued that warning in a cold voice as she tried to see what Baatesh was doing. He'd disassembled part of the bed frame, and she could see a flash of glowing green behind the metal panel he was replacing. She had no doubt that was the bomb.

Angry and rattled, she moved forward, pressing the gun to the base of his skull. She didn't know angrill physiology, but that was usually an effective spot on any species to neutralize them. "What do you think you're doing?"

He froze, his hands extended at his sides. "What I was paid to do."

"Why are you putting a bomb in Captain Wells's quarters, in her bed?" Baatesh hadn't moved, but Emily wasn't about to drop her guard. She pressed the gun more firmly against his skull when he failed to answer quickly enough.

With a wince, he said, "Again, that's what I was paid to do. I'm just following instructions."

"Instructions from whom?" Anthracite asked that question as he came closer, standing over Baatesh in a menacing fashion.

Baatesh didn't speak. Emily prodded deeper against his brainstem, her hand steady. "If you're not going to talk, then I have no reason to keep you alive. I could shoot you right now and explain it was resistance." Emily had no intention of doing any such thing, but she was proud how convincing she sounded when she uttered the threat.

It must've been enough to convince Baatesh, because he froze, his body stiffening, and he swallowed audibly. "You wouldn't."

She shoved in deeper, certain he was feeling the pain of the barrel now. "Try me. Explain yourself. Now."

"I was hired by a Jrojan ambassador to eliminate Prince Nykal and Hadley Wells."

"What is this ambassador's name?" Emily asked.

"Krill," said Hadley, suddenly appearing through the doorway as she stormed in. She had a gun of her own, and it was directed toward Baatesh as well. "Isn't that right? Ambassador Krill paid you to do this?"

Baatesh hesitated. "We didn't exchange names, but I'm certain I would recognize his voice if that will do for identification."

"You're going to cooperate?" asked Anthracite, his skepticism clear.

"I have a feeling cooperation will commute the death sentence, at least for me. Better the ambassador than me going to the chamber for this." Baatesh sounded unconcerned about betraying his client. So much for honor among thieves, though she wasn't certain that entirely applied to him. He was a thief, of course, but he was also a murderer. Or would've been if he'd had a chance. There was no telling how many other people he'd eliminated via similar jobs.

That would be for other security staff above her to sort out though. He was bound in leg irons and handcuffs within minutes of a large security detail arriving that included Hayes. Gordon looked as clueless as ever, and Emily was exasperated more than anything. She couldn't wait for the day he decided it was time to retire, since he wasn't good enough to be working in a position entrusted with the safety of everyone aboard.

The security detail started to prod Baatesh forward, but Anthracite stepped up, blocking the way for a moment. "Tell me if the angrills are planning to start a war again with the diabels?"

Baatesh looked genuinely surprised. "What gives you that impression? We're scattered, doing the best we can to get by. Who has time for war...at least yet?" Baatesh flashed him an arrogant grin as he added that part.

With a nod, Anthracite stepped aside, and the security agents herded Baatesh from the room as Nykal arrived.

"Hadley," he cried, sounding frantic as he rushed toward her. "Security contacted me to explain what's happening. Are you all right?" His hand went to the gentle swell of her belly as he asked.

"I am, though we still have to disassemble the bomb. I suggest we should all depart the room and leave that up to the experts." Hadley sounded surprisingly calm, though she was cradling her pregnant belly. "He meant to kill us."

"That white thing?" asked Nykal.

"Him too, but he claims to be working for an ambassador from Jroj." Nykal scowled. "Krill."

Hadley nodded, looking unsurprised. "No doubt. I thought he was done meddling, but apparently not."

Nykal put his arm around her waist, guiding Hadley out of the room ahead of them. "He will be now." Nykal was utterly convincing in his resolve, making Emily glad the captain had someone like him looking out for her.

She slanted a glance at Anth as they left the room. He'd been beside her every step of the way. Did that mean something? She hoped so, no longer wanting just something physical with the alien bartender. She'd much prefer forever.

Chapter Nine

HE TOOK EMILY'S HAND, leading her from the crew quarters and as far away from that sector as he could. The bar seemed safe enough, at least according to a rough mental calculation of the amount of materials Baatesh had stolen to create the bomb. It certainly would've taken out at least that corridor of crew quarters if it had exploded, but it was unlikely to go far beyond that, and safety protocols would've locked down hull breaches to keep the station stable in the event it exploded. He was reasonably confident in Olympus Station staff to be able to defuse the bomb, but he still wanted Emily out of any possible blast range.

When they reached the bar, Dahzhe look flustered. "I'm not any good at this. You have to take over."

Anthracite took the apron she handed him, but instead of putting it on, he raised his voice. "There's a bomb on the station. I suggest everyone return to their quarters, though avoid the station command crew quarters. The bar is officially closed."

There were some sounds of protest from the regulars, but mostly it was a stampede of feet rushing for the exit, and Anthracite closed the screen behind them. In the five years he'd run the bar here, it had never been closed, but they had the capability to do so, and he initiated the protocol without regret. If he got in trouble for closing the bar, so be it, though he couldn't imagine anyone would care under the circumstances. There were far more serious problems to deal with on Olympus Station now.

He returned to Emily, who'd taken a seat at one of the booths near the bar. He squeezed in beside her instead of sitting across from her, needing the reassurance of being able to feel her. He took her hand, and then he decided that wasn't enough, so he released it to put his arm around her shoulders and pull her closer against him. She didn't resist. Instead, she curled against him, soft and compliant, making it feel like his whole world was distilled in his arms.

"It was terrifying." Her voice trembled a little. "I never expected anything like that."

"Neither did I, but you handled it beautifully. You're very good at what you do, Emily."

She lifted her head from his shoulder, turning it enough to look up at him. "Thank you. I appreciated you not trying to take over and go ahead of me."

He'd never admit what a struggle that had been, but she'd handled herself with such competence, and she'd been the one the weapon. How could he do anything but trust her to handle it? "I knew you had everything under control."

She snorted. "It didn't feel like that exactly. I was sure he wasn't going to break and tell us anything. If he'd had a detonation device within reach, he could've set off the bomb and killed us all." She trembled a little. "His peaceful surrender was definitely not how I expected the day to end."

"He probably didn't bother to fight because he knew it was hopeless once security started looking for him." A chill of fear went through him as well when he realized what a close call they'd had, and it spurred him to hold her tighter. "The day's not over yet. There are still things we could do."

Her laugh was shaky. "I'm not sure I'm in the mood for anything like that."

"Such naughty thoughts," he teased, pushing back the fear. "I wasn't even thinking that." Anthracite wrapped his tail around her if thigh, needing to anchor himself. He had to know she was whole and in one piece, and he couldn't be too reassured of that. "I actually meant something more wholesome."

She tipped her head, eyeing him with surprise. "What did you have in mind?"

"I'd like to introduce you to my family. It would have to be via a comm videocall, of course, but I want them to know you. They'll appreciate getting a chance to become acquainted with you before I propose."

Her eyes widened. "Propose?"

He frowned. "Is that not the proper human term? My people call it *viratu*, but I think it's simply essentially the same. We pledge our souls to one another, entwining them in this life and any to follow. No doubt, we have already done so in countless lives before."

She still seemed hesitant. "Minus the reincarnation, it's roughly the same in translation. I just... Don't you think it's too soon?"

He flinched. "No, but I've been in love with you for almost a year. I understand I wasn't part of your world at all until recently."

She leaned forward, pressing a kiss to his neck. "I'm not saying I don't want to explore the possibility with you. I'd just like to slow down a little bit and see where we're headed. It'd be nice to enjoy the journey as much as the destination. Is that all right with you?"

For a moment, he was tempted to insist on a deeper connection, but he realized that would be unfair. He was confident she would soon catch up on her emotions, and they would be in a similar place, ready for the same level of commitment. "Of course, that's all right with me. I don't wish to rush or pressure you. I simply want to be with you under whatever circumstances you allow."

She chuckled, twisting until she was sitting on his lap. His tail had to disengage from her thigh, but he compensated by wrapping it around her waist again instead, pulling her nearer. "I'm not trying to control anything. I just want us to have a pace that allows us to get to know each other incredibly well before we go that far. I do have one stipulation though."

He braced himself. "What?"

"You have to stop the spying. I understand why you do it, but it puts me in a difficult position ethically. I don't want to have to report it to the commander, and I don't think I can hide it. If I have to tell him, you'll likely be transferred away from Olympus Station. It's also an unfair position to put you in, but—"

He put his finger against her lips. "It's an easy sacrifice to make. Timorith will be unhappy, but he'll understands." Anthracite didn't bother to reveal that he didn't care if his handler didn't really understand his choice. If Timorith had ever been in love, he was likely to sympathize.

If not, Anthracite was under no obligation to continue working for him in the role for which Timorith had recruited him. He wasn't going to be eliminated just because he stopped providing information. "People will still tell me things though. It's the nature of being a bartender."

She shrugged. "I'm not asking you to stop taking confidences. I just don't want to be in a position where I feel like I'm betraying the station and my position as a security agent."

He nodded. "I understand, and you have my word that the spying ceases today. I'll contact Timorith, and it's over."

She cupped his face in her hands. "Will you be safe, or will he take it badly?"

He smiled. "You don't have to worry about him killing me for refusing to continue to pass along information. Our species rarely resorts to violence these days, having learned a lot from nearly mutual genocide with the angrills."

"In that case, I don't see any reason why we can't be together and determine where we're heading." Her mouth touched his, and the kiss quickly grew from one of gentle persuasion to passion.

When they pulled apart several moments later, both breathing heavily, he said, "You aren't in the mood?"

She grinned. "Things change, Anthracite."

Epilogue

EMILY STOOD PROUDLY as Captain Wells pinned on her new stripes before draping the medal over her neck. She was receiving a promotion and acknowledgment of vital service provided to save the station. Anthracite stood beside her, and he soon accepted a similar medal from Hadley.

Emily couldn't keep from beaming, and when she looked at Gordon, who stood toward the back of the crowd, her grin grew a little wider. She now outranked him, so the next time he tried his half-assed security efforts, she'd be able to rein him in and make him do it the right way. At most, he'd put up a fuss, but he'd comply.

After the pinning and medal ceremony, they mingled among the partygoers for a while, until Anthracite maneuvered her close to the window that offered an expansive view of the space around them. She leaned against him, enjoying this quiet moment among the celebration. It was just the two of them. It was the perfect time, though she'd anticipated waiting until later. "I'd like to meet your family now, since I'm ready for *viratu* too."

His eyes widened. "Are you proposing to me, Emily Ipsy?"

She grinned. "I am, Anthracite. Will you be my husband?"

He nodded enthusiastically as he pulled her closer, kissing her passionately. She pressed back against him, her mouth curving to his, and she almost forgot where they were for a moment. Fortunately, Anthracite seemed to have a little more awareness, and he gently pushed her way after a long moment. "That will have to wait until we're back in our quarters." He had moved in with her a couple of weeks ago.

She cleared her throat and looked around. "Yes, I suppose you're right. It would be scandalous to proceed from here."

He waved to the crowd. "Should we tell them this has become a *viratu* celebration as well?"

Emily hesitated and then shook her head. "Soon, but I'd like to savor this moment for just you and me."

If he was disappointed, he didn't show it. "That's perfectly fine with me as well. I love you, Emily."

She leaned closer, clinging tightly to him again. "I love you too, Anthracite." She kissed him then, once more losing herself in his mouth and no longer caring who was around.

It was just the two of them celebrating this momentous event, and the rest of the world ceased to exist in that second. The world revolving around and cocooning the two of them felt right and proper, like everything was in balance and as it should be. How could it be anything else with Anthracite at her side? Maybe there was something to his belief they had lived lifetimes together before, because he certainly felt familiar.

Not comfortable though. Things were passionate and exciting with Anthracite. If she'd known him before, she looked forward to remembering everything there was to know about him in the future as they lived this life together.

About Aurelia

AURELIA SKYE IS THE pen name *USA Today* bestselling author Kit Tunstall uses when writing science fiction romance. It's simply a way to separate the myriad types of stories she writes so readers know what to expect with each "author."

Did you love *Security Agent's Alien Bartender*? Then you should read *Cybernetic Hearts: Complete Series*[1] by Aurelia Skye!

Celestial Mates Agent Freydon Rote sets in motion four mate pairings in the Cybernetic Hearts series. It all begins when he brings modern-day human Carrie four centuries into the future, where she finds a ravaged planet and a war between humans and cyborgs—and also the love of her life in the cyborg general, DVS84. Their match is the catalyst for cyborgs JSN42, MX, and RVN to find their human mates while finding a way to end the war between the cyborgs and humans while fighting their mutual enemy, the synths.

The complete collection includes:

"Mated To The Cyborg General"

"Claimed By The Cyborg Commander"

---

1. https://books2read.com/u/b6Mr9W

2. https://books2read.com/u/b6Mr9W

"Fated For the Cyborg Officer"
"Meant For The Cyborg Captain"
"Baby For The Cyborg General"

Also by Aurelia Skye

Alien Baby Pact
Baby For The Brundle Commander
Baby For The Grimlock General
Baby For The Palantir Chief
Baby For The Alphan Captain

Celestial Mates
Wrong Place, Right Mate
Destined For The Drakari Warlords

Cybernetic Hearts
Mated To The Cyborg General
Claimed By The Cyborg Commander
Fated For The Cyborg Officer
Meant For The Cyborg Captain
Baby For The Cyborg General
Cybernetic Hearts: Complete Series

Dazon Agenda
Written In The Stars
Alien's Babies
Diplomatic Affairs
Moon Madness
Across The Stars
Emperor's Assassin Bride
Dazon Agenda: Complete Collection

Future Fairytales
Hooked

Harrow Bay
Hell Gates & Hot Flashes
Nightmares & Night Sweats
Warlocks & Wrinkles
Love Spells & Liver Spots
Phantasms & Presbyopia
Vampires & Varicose Veins
Mermaids & Mood Swings
Séances & Sagging Skin
Necromancy & Knee Pains
Marids & Memory Loss
Devil Deals & Dizzy Spells
Happy Endings & New Beginnings
Harrow Bay, Volume 1
Hellhounds & Mistletoe
Harrow Bay, Volume 2

Harrow Bay, Volume 3

Hell Virus
Catching Hell
Surviving Hell
Bleeding Hell
Raising Hell
Sharing Hell

Howls Romance
The Jaguar Alpha's Forbidden Lover

Northstar Shifters
Northstar Heir's Scarred Mate

Olympus Station
Station Commander's Surrogate
Alien Prince's Secret Baby
Security Agent's Alien Bartender
Olympus Station Compilation

SpicyShorts
Music In My Heart
Kilted Tentacle Monster: A Search for True Love

Sweet Escapes
Hook & Wendy

Three Crones Inn
Vastly Inn-proved
Ghastly Intentions
Ghostly Inn-heritance
Three Crones Inn Compilation

True North
True North #1: Death & Deception
True North #2: Rescued & Revelations
True North #3: Fire & Ice
True North #4: Enemies & Lovers
True North #5: Truth & Tiranog
True North #6: Fight & Flight
True North #7: Love & Loss

Wounded Warriors
Relentless
Marked
Justice
Wounded Warriors Collection
Hunted